D0633614

POOR MR NIBBLE

This edition first published in the United Kingdom in 1999 by
Brockhampton Press
20 Bloomsbury Street
London WC1B 3QA
a member of the Hodder Headline PLC Group

Designed and Produced for Brockhampton Press by
Open Door Limited
80 High Street, Colsterworth, Lincolnshire, NG33 5JA

Illustrator: F. Stocks May
Colour separation: GA Graphics Stamford

Title: BLACKBERRY FARM, Poor Mr Nibble
ISBN: 1-84186-014-X

POOR MR NIBBLE

Jane Pilgrim

Illustrated by F. Stocks May

BROCKHAMPTON PRESS

Poor Mr Nibble felt ill. Poor Mr Nibble had a stiff neck. Poor Mr Nibble had a sore throat.

Mrs Nibble was very worried about him and asked Ernest Owl to come. Ernest Owl listened very carefully to what she told him. He looked very carefully at Mr Nibble and then he said: “Mumps!” He turned to Mrs Nibble and said: “Mumps!” And then he looked once more at Mr Nibble and said: “Mumps! Definitely!”

Mr Nibble was very, very upset. It was the show at Blackberry Farm the next day, and he had some very fine carrots and lettuces in his garden. Who would show them for him?

Mrs Nibble had her pots of home-made jam to take. Rosy, Posy and Christopher each had their handwork from school. There would be no one to take Mr Nibble's carrots and lettuces. Mr Nibble was very upset and sighed deeply.

Mrs Nibble was very upset too, because she knew that Mr Nibble's carrots and lettuces were very good. But she could not carry everything. She stood in the doorway looking out at the garden and tried to think what to do. Suddenly she knew and was happy.

She put Rosy, Posy and Christopher to bed early that night. She gave Mr Nibble a hot drink and tucked him up and drew the curtains. And then she crept out of the house.

Down the path she went. Into the little shed to fetch a basket, and then she pulled the six best carrots and the six best lettuces and crept across the field to the big oak tree where Ernest Owl lived.

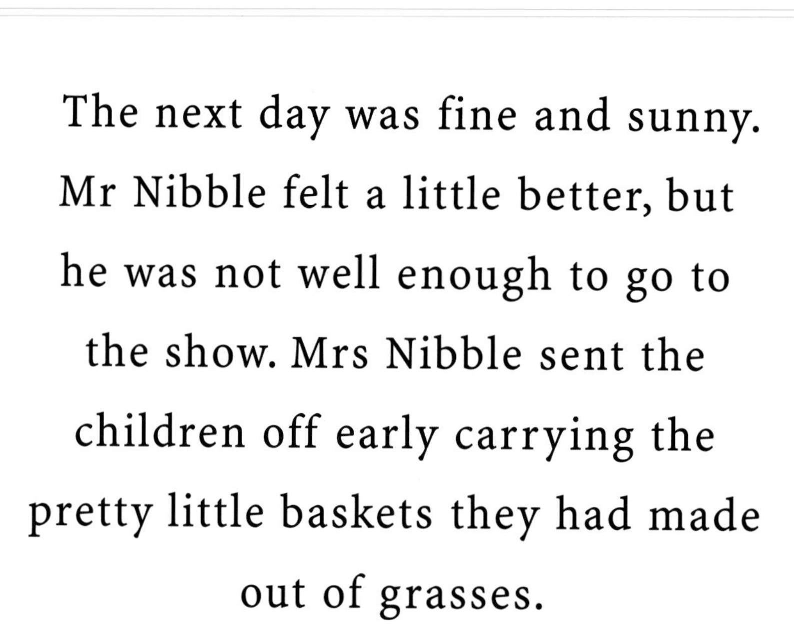

The next day was fine and sunny. Mr Nibble felt a little better, but he was not well enough to go to the show. Mrs Nibble sent the children off early carrying the pretty little baskets they had made out of grasses.

She picked up her basket of jams and kissed Mr Nibble goodbye. "Don't be sad about your carrots and lettuces," she said, "I will come back as soon as I can. Lucy Mouse will come and give you your dinner." And off she went.

Lucy Mouse came in and gave Mr Nibble his dinner. She had been to the show early. "There are some very good lettuces and carrots there," she told him. "But I don't know where they came from." Mr Nibble sighed.

At tea-time Joe Robin flew in. "Fine lot of stuff at the show, Mr Nibble," he called. "Best lettuces and carrots I've ever seen. They are going to give the prizes very soon." Poor Mr Nibble felt more and more sad. If only he had been able to take his lettuces and carrots. Surely they would have been the best in the show? He had never grown such splendid ones.

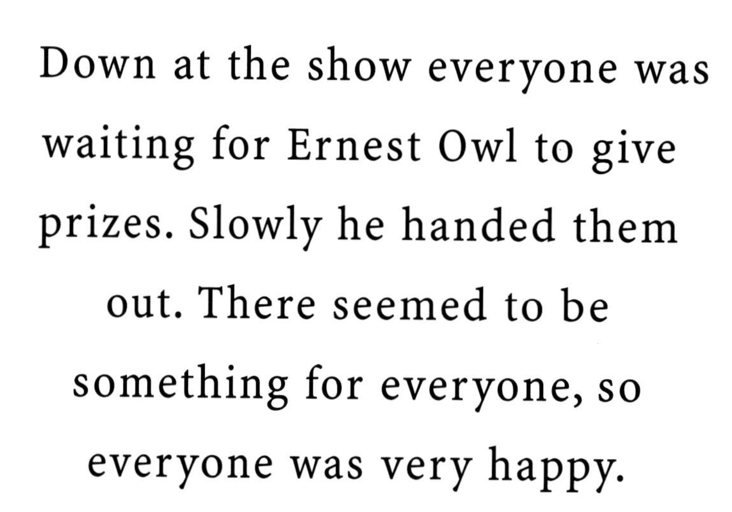

Down at the show everyone was waiting for Ernest Owl to give prizes. Slowly he handed them out. There seemed to be something for everyone, so everyone was very happy.

Then Ernest Owl gave Mrs Nibble an extra prize. "For Mr Nibble," he explained, "for the finest lettuces and carrots in the show, and we all hope that his mumps are better." And everyone cheered very loudly, because they had all been very sorry for Mr Nibble. Mrs Nibble ran all the way home. Her plan had worked. Ernest Owl had kept Mr Nibble's lettuces and carrots safe all night so that they would be in the show in the morning. She was very happy.

Mr Nibble was quite overcome with excitement and surprise. He hugged Mrs Nibble and said: "You are the best and the cleverest wife in the world! How lucky I am to have you and Rosy, Posy and Christopher, as well as the finest lettuces and carrots at Blackberry Farm." And he felt so much better that he got up for supper.